Dear Parent:
Your child's love of reading starts here!

Every child learns to read in a different way and at his or her own speed. Some go back and forth between reading levels and read favorite books again and again. Others read through each level in order. You can help your young reader improve and become more confident by encouraging his or her own interests and abilities. From books your child reads with you to the first books he or she reads alone, there are I Can Read Books for every stage of reading:

SHARED READING
Basic language, word repetition, and whimsical illustrations, ideal for sharing with your emergent reader

BEGINNING READING
Short sentences, familiar words, and simple concepts for children eager to read on their own

READING WITH HELP
Engaging stories, longer sentences, and language play for developing readers

READING ALONE
Complex plots, challenging vocabulary, and high-interest topics for the independent reader

ADVANCED READING
Short paragraphs, chapters, and exciting themes for the perfect bridge to chapter books

I Can Read Books have introduced children to the joy of reading since 1957. Featuring award-winning authors and illustrators and a fabulous cast of beloved characters, I Can Read Books set the standard for beginning readers.

A lifetime of discovery begins with the magical words "I Can Read!"

Visit www.icanread.com for information
on enriching your child's reading experience.

The New Pony

Pony Scouts: The New Pony. Copyright © 2013 by HarperCollins Publishers. All rights reserved. Manufactured in China. No part of this book may be used or reproduced in any manner without written permission except in the case of brief quotations embodied in critical articles and reviews. For information address HarperCollins Children's Books, a division of HarperCollins Publishers, 10 East 53rd Street, New York, NY 10022.
www.icanread.com

Library of Congress catalog card number: 2012943204
ISBN 978-0-06-208674-7 (trade bdg.)—ISBN 978-0-06-208673-0 (pbk.)
Typography by Sean Boggs

12 13 14 15 16 SCP 10 9 8 7 6 5 4 3 2 1 ❖ First Edition

PONY SCOUTS

The New Pony

by Catherine Hapka
pictures by Anne Kennedy

HARPER

An Imprint of HarperCollinsPublishers

Jill lived on a pony farm.

One Saturday, Meg and Annie,

her best friends, came over.

Jill, Meg, and Annie

called themselves the Pony Scouts.

"I'm afraid your riding lesson

will be delayed today, girls,"

Jill's mom told them.

"Oh, no!" Meg cried. "Why?"

Jill's mom smiled at the girls.

"Because a new pony

is arriving at the farm today."

"What's his name?" Annie asked.

"His name is Taffy," Jill's mom said.

A trailer pulled in
with a palomino pony on it.
Taffy was the cutest pony
the Pony Scouts had ever seen!

Jill's mom put Taffy in a paddock.

He ran around and whinnied loudly.

"He seems nervous," Annie said.

"He's young and still green,"
Jill's mom told her.

Meg giggled. "Green?" she said.

"He looks yellowish gold to me!"
Jill explained, "Green means
that a pony isn't fully trained yet."

"That's right," Jill's mom said.
"I hope Jill will help me
finish Taffy's training."
Jill was super excited to help.

One week later,

it was time for another lesson.

"Do you want to ride Taffy today?"

Jill's mom asked her.

"Definitely!" Jill said.

Jill led Taffy into the practice ring.

"I'll help you mount, Jill,"
her mom said.

"I know how to mount
by myself," Jill said.

"Yes," her mom replied,
"but Taffy is new to this,
remember?"
She held Taffy's bridle
while Jill got on.

Then Jill's mom turned

to help Annie adjust her stirrups.

"Let's go, Taffy," Jill said.

She nudged his sides with both legs

to get him to walk.

But Taffy just stood there.

"What's the matter?" Meg asked.

"Nothing," Jill said.

She knew what to do

when a pony was feeling lazy.

17

"Walk, Taffy!" Jill ordered.

Then she gave the pony

a sharp kick in the side.

Taffy let out a snort of surprise.

Then he burst into a gallop!

"Whoa!" Jill cried.

She pulled back on the reins,

but Taffy just ran faster!

Jill hardly ever got scared

when she was riding.

But she was scared now!

It felt as if the pony

might never stop running!

"Relax, Jill!" Jill's mom called.

"Talk to him!"

"Easy, Taffy," Jill said.

"Slow down, boy. Please?"

The pony pricked an ear
in Jill's direction.
She kept talking to him.
Soon he slowed to a canter
and then to a trot.

"Give and take with the reins,"

Jill's mom called.

Jill did as her mom said.

Finally Taffy stopped.

"What happened?" Jill's mom asked.

"He was being lazy," Jill said.

"So I kicked him harder.

Then he ran away with me!"

Jill's mom shook her head.

"He wasn't being lazy," she said.

"He just didn't understand

what you wanted him to do.

You have to be patient with him."

"Ready to try again?" her mom asked.

"I don't know," Jill said.

Riding a green pony was harder

and scarier than she'd expected.

"You can do it, Jill," her mom said.
"Just remember how it feels
not to know so much about riding."
"Like us!" Meg put in,
and Annie nodded.

That made Jill smile.

She'd helped her friends

learn to ride.

Could she help Taffy

learn to be ridden, too?

"Okay, let's try again," she said.

"Walk on, Taffy," Jill said.

She urged him on with her legs.

He didn't move,

so she asked him again—gently.

This time he started walking!

Meg and Annie cheered.

"Nicely done," Jill's mom said.

Jill smiled and patted Taffy.

Training Taffy wasn't going to be

as easy as she'd expected,

but it was going to be fun!

PONY POINTERS

palomino: a horse or pony that has a golden-colored body and a white mane and tail

green: a horse or pony that isn't fully trained yet

mounting: getting onto a horse or pony

gallop: the fastest gait— racehorses race at a gallop